T.D. Luong (Thang Dac) was born on 21 March 1971, the Year of the Pig, during the Vietnam War. The Year of the Pig is considered to be a lucky year in Vietnamese culture and he considers himself very lucky because he came to Australia as a refugee with his family on 20 June 1975, shortly after the war ended on 30 April 1975. Thang's father, Hai Ngoc Luong, was a persecuted journalist during the war (1945–1975) and died, at age 91, on 2 February 2006. Since that time, Thang has reflected on the impact of war on his family. He is currently working on a novel inspired by his late father. Thang holds a Bachelor of Arts in Communication (with a journalism major) and a Masters of Arts in Creative Writing from the University of Technology, Sydney. He also holds a Bachelor of Laws from the University of New South Wales and is a solicitor of the NSW Supreme Court. He is married and the father of two great kids. Thang grew up in, and loved, the Inner West of Sydney in the 1980s (a decade he finds hard to relinquish). He has previously done freelance journalism and currently works as a lawyer. *Refugee Wolf* is his first published work of fiction. Join him on Facebook at www.facebook.com/Thang.D.Luong.88 Or visit his blog at www.flyingpigblogdotcom.com

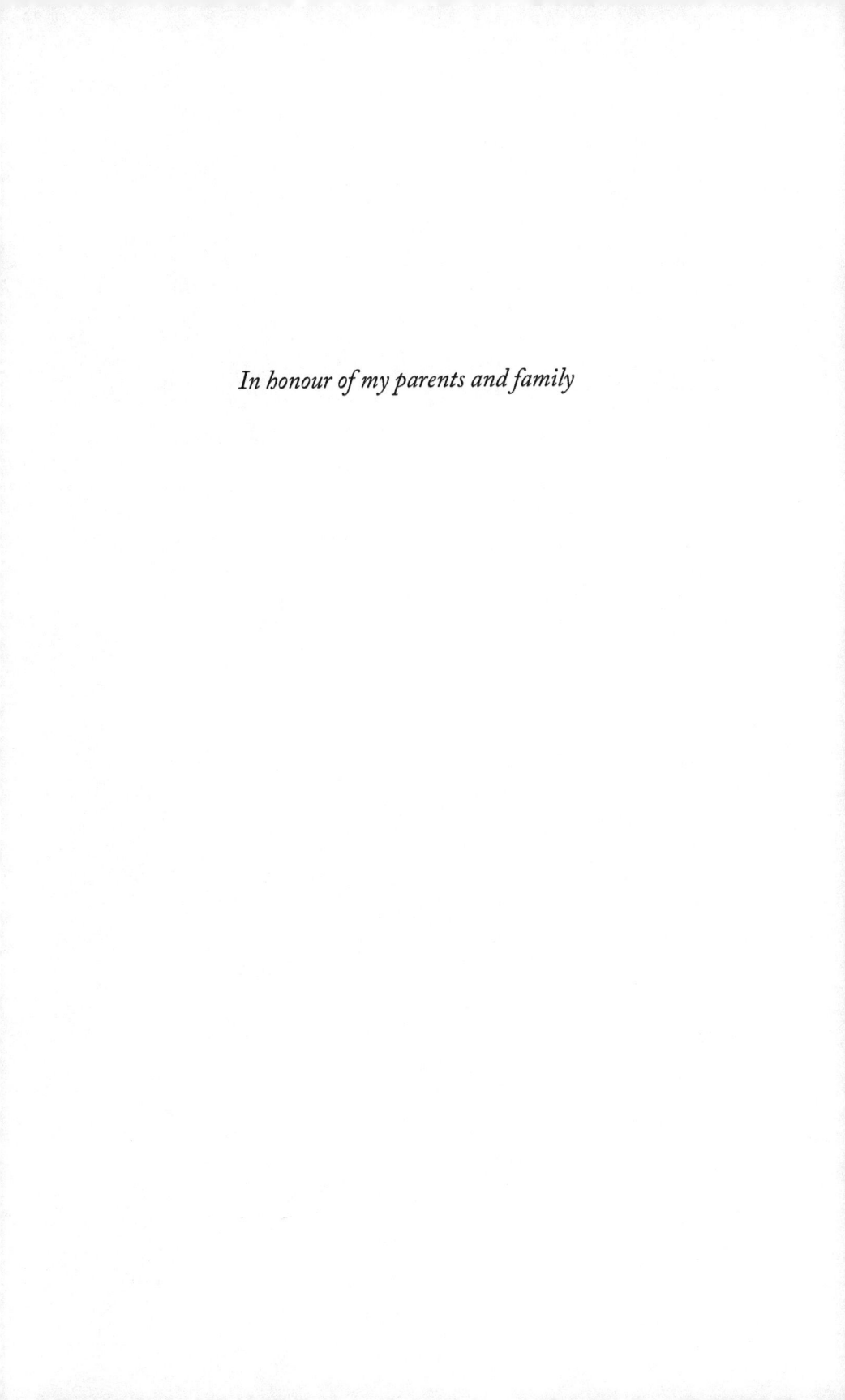

In honour of my parents and family

REFUGEE WOLF

T.D. LUONG

First published 2013 in Australia by Flying Pig Media
Reprinted in 2014
Reprinted in 2017
Copyright © T.D. Luong 2013
ISBN: 978-0-9922815-4-0 (paperback)
The moral right of the author has been asserted.

Cataloguing-in-publication data for *Refugee Wolf* is available from the
National Library of Australia.

Printed in the U.S.A by Createspace 2017
Cover illustration and design by Roy Chen, www.xoum.com.au
Typeset in Adobe Caslon Pro by Rod Morrison, www.xoum.com.au

Contents

Author's Note

I am a Vietnamese-Australian and do not speak on behalf of the Vietnamese-Australian community, many of whom have refugee backgrounds, nor any refugees from other backgrounds, in any way.

This story uses satire to highlight a serious issue and I acknowledge the traumatic journey of all asylum seekers and refugees. It is not my intention to undermine their feelings and experiences.

The first wave of Vietnamese "Boat People" fled from the authorities because of a well-grounded fear of being persecuted after the end of the Vietnam War on 30 April 1975. My late dad, a journalist, was one of these people.

This short story was inspired by Michael

Jackson's song "Bad"[1] and the fairytale, *The Three Little Pigs*.

The song's lyrics had a double meaning. It was implied that there was something inherently cool or good about the main character and his associates who were, in the music video clip, dressed up in street chic. At the same time, all of the characters were presented as being from the "bad" part of town, and their predisposition being something other than good.

The Three Little Pigs fairytale has many versions. With its moral code about how the world works — that in order to succeed, three heads are better than one — it has been re-told, re-interpreted and re-invented in a number of ways. I have re-invented the fairytale as speculative/science fiction, and mixed it with dark comedy in the context of asylum seekers.

No character in the story is based on any single, real person. The story is a reflection of the many diverse and contrasting views in society. The statements and messages contained in the story are prevalent on the internet.

Australia is a signatory to the United Nations Convention relating to the Status of Refugees (CRSR), established in 1951.

I have quoted various provisions under the

CRSR so that readers become familiar with them, if they are not already.

Article 1 of the Convention, as amended by the 1967 Protocol, provides the definition of a refugee:

> *"A person who owing to a well-founded fear of being persecuted for reasons of race, religion, nationality, membership of a particular social group or political opinion, is outside the country of his nationality and is unable or, owing to such fear, is unwilling to avail himself of the protection of that country; or who, not having a nationality and being outside the country of his former habitual residence as a result of such events, is unable or, owing to such fear, is unwilling to return to it . . ."*

Article 31 deals with the issue of penalties if an asylum seeker has entered a contracting state's territory without legal authorisation:

> *"The Contracting States shall not impose penalties, on account of their illegal entry or presence, on refugees who, coming directly from a territory where their life or freedom was threatened in the sense of article 1, enter or are*

present in their territory without authorization,
provided they present themselves without delay
to the authorities and show good cause for their
illegal entry or presence."

Article 33 deals with the issue of not sending an asylum seeker back to their place of persecution. This is known as the principle of refoulement, or no forcible return:

"No Contracting State shall expel or return
('refouler') a refugee in any manner whatsoever
to the frontiers of territories where his life or
freedom would be threatened on account of his
race, religion, nationality, membership of a
particular social group or political opinion."

I do not profess to be an expert on the asylum seeker matter. The issues are complex and I encourage people to research them and reflect upon how their own distant relatives came to live in Australia. Naturally, I would like people to express their valid concerns through robust and thoughtful discussion.

T.D. Luong

REFUGEE WOLF

Chapter 1

To the Planet of Straw

Once upon a time, in 2500 AD, I was sitting in a dunny of a jail cell. Mate, it stank like wolf manure. I licked my right paw, then ripped a fart. The guards laughed like a bunch of kookaburras. I laughed too, but I shouldn't have.

You see, I was a refugee, and wrongly jailed and persecuted for eating too many pigs. The flamin' humans had used me. I had been hired by the Anti-Mutant Pig Company and had to kill and eat about fifty per day. Earth had been overrun by mutant pigs from outta space which had landed out the back of Woop Woop.

Mr Bacon — which I thought was a funny name — the head supervisor, had accused me of eating more than my fair share. Which simply wasn't true. It'd been a set-up so they could out-source my services to other wolves prepared to work for less. They had convicted me under the *Excessive Eating Act*. Well, anyhow, that's how I came to be on death row.

But despite all of this, I still loved my bacon, especially Vietnamese pork bread rolls.

My plan was to escape from The Island, near Ostraya, in the middle of nowhere. I wanted to go to the Planet of Straw, the Planet of Sticks[2] or the Planet of McSpaceMansions. There were rumours that these planets were controlled by We The Piggery Inc., a company made up of a bunch of super hungry pigs. One of them had commissioned the invention of a pill known as Excess. Apparently, everyday over a gazillion pills were crushed and mixed into the water system which made all of the pigs living on these planets consume too much. Excess made them think warm and fuzzy thoughts. And, of course, the super hungry pigs became super rich after they sold the pills to the humans. There was also a conspiracy theory going around that the super hungry pigs weren't really in control at all. The minority shareholders — every other pig on these planets — were supposedly pulling the strings through dodgy deals with the super hungry pigs. Either way, I suspected that all of them just loved being high on Excess. While I couldn't confirm these rumours, I was hopeful of getting asylum 'cos a couple of my mates had been granted it. But that depended on which of the planets was going to accept me under the *Inter-Galactic Law to Protect Refugee Wolves from Humans.*

I couldn't remember how long I'd been in jail. Yes, I could. No, wait a sec, no I couldn't.

Anyway, I had them fixed up. What those guards didn't know was that there were some ex-terrorists who could help my escape. They were smugglers, now, and had hijacked a space shuttle for use in their trade.

You see, in these happy and laid-back times, the humans had failed to respond to a big black hole at the edge of the universe which had sucked almost every galaxy into its path. This meant that there was nowhere else but the three planets I could escape to.

I stood up on my hind legs and paced about the jail cell. I went to the mirror. I had this fat gut because I had downed those mutant pigs and plenty of six-packs of beer. Each tinny had a button on it. When you pressed it, the tinny would vaporise and then I'd inhale the amber vapour through my snout.

My smelly brown fur hadn't been washed in weeks. I was wearing my favourite light blue tracky dax. It was made from weird synthetic stuff that wouldn't rip. I had forgotten something. I checked my right pocket and in it was a Pokies-In-Space chip — worth a gazillion dollars — which I had won ages ago on my favourite poker machine at the club. That was good, just in case I needed it if I got into trouble.

I didn't wear undies 'cos my farts had stained them too much. I had a sudden itchy twitch in my bum — worms. So I started clenching my bum cheeks — in, out, in, out. Then, I paced about the cell to distract myself but I felt the buggers gnawing away.

Hey, I wasn't that bad looking. I really loved my four fangs. My snout was a bit crooked 'cos I used to get into a heap of blues on Friday nights. I guess I took after my great great great great great great great great granddaddy who used to bash up a few meatheads — on the SCG Hill — at the cricket. I had heard that way back then, the Hill was a place where there was fraternising between us and the yobbos. Ah, the good ol' days.

I wanted to see a disciple of the Masterful Healer, just in case the escape went down the dunny hole. One of the guards unlocked the gates with a remote control and escorted me to the visitor's cell, down the corridor. They carried laser guns. The cell was divided by neon pink glowing bars, which could apparently zap you to death. He was on the other side, sitting on a chair behind a table that floated in the air. The guards stood near him. He was bald and wore a white designer pair of silk tracky dax. He gave me the once over with his droopy eyes.

"Hello," he said. "How are you, son?"

"Well, um, I've been thinking . . . about why those humans turned on me . . ."

"What's your name, son?"

"Big Bad Ben," I said.

"Look, there's no rhyme nor reason, my son," he said. "The Masterful Healer made us human beings intelligent, rational and compassionate, but in his heart of hearts, he reckons most of us consume too much."

"Look, I thought about giving up pork once," I said.

"That's an admirable thought . . . what's your name again?" he said, while yawning.

"Big Bad Ben."

"*Big Bad Ben?* Really? That's a nice name, son . . . well now's the time to change your ways. Have you tried converting to vegetarianism?"

Didn't he *know* I loved my pork? I was a *wolf* for cryin' out loud.

"That sounds alright," I said, with my eyebrows half-raised, in disbelief. "What does the Masterful Healer think about wolves?"

"Oh, the Masterful Healer loves your kind. The Masterful Healer made one of you appear in *The Ancient Text of Healing* that featured a parable called *The Three Little Pigs*."

"You're pullin' my leg, right?"

"'Course not. The moral of the story was to not covet McSpaceMansions otherwise a Big Bad Wolf might blow it down."

There was probably some hidden message in there but buggered if I knew what the story was about. Anyway, this guy could've quoted *The Ancient Text of Healing* until he was blue in the face but it wasn't going to get me help out of here. My ears turned red and my blood boiled. So I growled. Grrr . . .

The disciple's right, droopy eye twitched and his

hands shook. I quickly calmed down 'cos those guards looked trigger happy.

"Got be going," he said. "Good chatting to you, Big Bad Ben."

"You too." *Not.*

The guards took me back to the jail cell. They had stuffed me with cans of baked beans. The toxic gas was building up. I could do deadly farts. I reckoned that eating all those mutant pigs from outta space had put some alien bacteria in my gut. But I couldn't let one fly 'cos my worms were blocking my bum. My stomach muscles tightened and I managed to let off a pretty smelly one. No one died but they collapsed in a heap.

Lucky there was a guard who flopped over near me. He had the keys to the cell and I let myself out. I gave the keys to another wolf and it unlocked the doors of the cells where the other wolves were.

One of the guards was still semi-conscious. He fired his laser gun. Red beams smashed against cement walls and dust scattered everywhere. We bolted towards the front door but laser beams flew in all directions. So we ducked and weaved and crawled along the ground. Clumps of loose and dead fur fell off our backs.

It floated in the air for an instant, before falling to the ground.

One of the wolves smashed a glass box, near the front door, which covered a button. The wolf pressed it and the pink-coloured laser fence surrounding the jail disappeared. That button was there for emergencies in case the humans had to escape from *us*. We all managed to escape.

There was a rust bucket of a space shuttle lying on a gravelly tarmac surrounded by a grey, limp forest, near the coast of The Island. There were quite a lot of tiles missing from the space shuttle. As I went up the steps to enter the door, a man with dark, curly hair and a long beard greeted me. He was one of the ex-terrorists. Everyone on board was human, except us wolves. He handed me a spacesuit with a few holes in it and I put it on.

As I took my seat, I noticed there wasn't much room. It seated no more than ten wolves, max. But about fifty of us were crammed in.

One of the ex-terrorists, the flight attendant, walked by and warned us not to relieve ourselves while up in space 'cos it would get kinda messy. She walked over to me and I asked, "Is this thing safe?"

"Of course, don't worry," she said. "Once we're up, the ones not strapped in will float around — that's how we can cram more of you guys in."

"Gotta make a few quid, eh?" I said.

She nodded her head.

I was strapped in, and was lucky enough to grab a seat with in-flight entertainment. I pressed the button on the screen in front of me. A 3D hologram materialised with a menu of great re-runs. Some of my favourite Kung Fu films were there, like *Chop Socky Wolf*. Beauty. It was going to take half a day to get to the Planet of Straw, so I tried to relax into my seat.

We took off. I slept and dreamt about my itchy bum and gigantic worms eating me alive.

When I woke up, we had landed. I looked out of the window and saw out in the distance heaps of houses made of straw. Some houses were tall, others squat. What a stinking pigsty. I took off the spacesuit. I could smell their poo even though the door of the space shuttle wasn't opened yet. Once it was open, I walked down the stairs onto the tarmac and noticed even more tiles had fallen off the space shuttle.

The flight attendant was kind of giving me the eye.

"You should fix those tiles," I said.

"Yeah, I know," she said, half-dejected. "Times are a bit tough. See, we're going through a bit of a restructure. Now we have to refinance some of our part-time bombing ventures."

"Strewth, times *are* tough."

"Go to the hangar," she said. "They'll process your application there."

The hangar was like a huge metal vault, with gigantic glass windows. On the horizon there were thousands of houses made of straw. Hovering in mid-air was a big LCD screen, with a message with white letters on a black background, which read:

BEWARE OF REFUGEE WOLVES WHICH SAY LET ME IN, LET ME IN . . .

As I walked towards the checkpoint there were yellow arrows painted on the ground. The arrows pointed towards words painted in white saying:

SEE-THROUGH CONVEYOR BELT APPROACHING

I walked onto the conveyor belt which was

made of a tough but flexible, clear resin and looked down into a cellar. There appeared to be skeletons of other wolves. Strewth, what happened to them? At the end of the walkway, I queued up behind some of the other wolves. There was another smaller LCD screen with another message hovering near several pigs processing the applications at various counters. The message said:

BEER DRINKERS TO THE LEFT, NON-BEER DRINKERS TO THE RIGHT

As I was making my way to the left-hand side, a couple of the security guards standing near the pig at the counter gave me the evil eye like I was an alien. All of the other wolves went to the right-hand side. I went to the side counter and filled in an electronic form on a LCD screen. It had a green glow and was probably full of radiation. The ratbags were trying to get rid of me even before I got into their planet! Then, I heard on the PA system an announcement:

"HOORAY! HOORAY! Our Dear Inter-Planetary Bouncer, Omni-Vortexa, plans to import more uranium from Earth!"

Huh? Who? Was that for the LCD screen?

Then, I walked up to the counter. The pig wore a shiny black jumpsuit.

"*Behind* the line," the pig said, pointing to a mark that was two metres back from the counter. I moved back. "Don't want to catch any diseases, you know. Have you done your form?"

"Yeah."

On the form was a question about how many tinnies I consumed per day. I lied and wrote one. In front of the pig was a see-through pane that hovered in mid-air. The pig touched it and various icons of aliens bobbed up on the screen. There was an icon that looked liked a wolf. The pig pressed the screen a few more times and it shook its head.

"Liar," the pig said.

"What?"

"Our computer has links to a computer on Earth. The database has a lot of videos of your family from over the centuries."

"So?"

"Well, there's footage of your relatives standing on the SCG Hill chucking beer bottles, vomiting, getting into punch-ups . . ."

"But you've got nothing on me, right?"

"Oh, yes we do. Before you went to jail on Earth, hidden cameras were set up in your lair and caught you consuming more than a case per day."

"Strewth — that was my mate, Bazza," I said,

scratching my head as I stared into the distance. "Or was it Wuzza?"

Truth of the matter was I didn't remember.

"Doesn't matter."

"Just because I hang out with a bunch of drunks doesn't mean I'm one," I said.

I was going to huff and puff but held back. I noticed there were pigs dressed in black security uniforms crawling all over the place. They carried laser guns.

"*Crikey*, mate, can I see your manager?" I said.

"No — we don't want good-for-nothing beer swilling louts. Try your luck on the Planet of Sticks!"

At this point, my head vibrated. Flamin' pig made me feel like changing into a werewolf even though technically I wasn't one. My ears went all red but my fangs weren't extending in a hurry. Sometimes I wished I had the power to turn into a werewolf. Imagine that . . .

"You know, normally, I would huff and puff and blow your house down, but *stuff* the lot of youse," I said, and walked with my tail between my legs towards the space shuttle.

Chapter One: To the Planet of Straw

Questions for consideration

1. What is your impression of the main character, Big Bad Ben, the refugee wolf? Why do you feel fear or sympathy towards him? How is fear or sympathy expressed towards refugees and / or immigrants in your society?

2. How is the dystopian world set up in terms of time and place?

3. Which kind of story telling techniques are used in the story? For example, discuss the use of fairy tales, allegory, satire, symbolism, anthropomorphism and voice.

Chapter 2

To the Planet of Sticks

As we were landing on the Planet of Sticks, from out of my window, I saw thousands and thousands of houses made out of sticks.

I was alone now, except for the crew. All of the wolves that were with me had been granted asylum on the Planet of Straw 'cos they didn't drink beer. The flight attendant, again, gave me the eye. "Good luck," she said.

While walking down the stairs onto the tarmac, I picked up the scent of other animals and their poo. *Hmmm.* Strange. It smelt like a zoo and was a bigger pigsty than the Planet of Straw. There was manure and all sorts of droppings all over the tarmac. Some ratbag had sold me the raw prawn. The flight attendant told me that this planet had once been a detention camp for refugees who'd jumped the queue. I might have been one on the run but I still wanted to live in a nice place. Who didn't?

The processing area looked the same as the hangar on the Planet of Straw. There was the same LCD screen with a message about watching out for refugee wolves. I went up to the side counter to fill in another form on the LCD screen, which had the same green glow. *Conspiracy!* I started to feel a bit nauseous. Maybe those gamma rays were melting my stomach. Anyway, I didn't want to give up and stop. I went up to the check-in counter and stood behind a yellow line. There was a pig behind it wearing a black military-style bomber jacket. Behind the pig was a LCD screen hovering near its head which read:

HAPPY AS A PIG IN MUD (BUT WE'RE SCARED OF BEING SWAMPED BY REFUGEE WOLVES!!!)

"Nice message," I said. *Not.* This place stank of all sorts of manure.

"Thanks, we really love it here," the pig said. Then, the pig looked at the screen in front of it. "So who do we have here, Mr Wolf?"

On the form were questions like how violent I was in certain situations. For example, what was my procedure for eating pigs, and what kind of chomping techniques did I like best?

I said I was, "the Baddest Wolf of them all."

The pig laughed and said, "Yeah right. Hey, have you read a great book called *The Inter-Galactic Naysayers?*"

"Nah," I said.

"Well, you can't be that bad, then. The story's about a bunch of super hungry pigs from the Top Twenty Planets of Excess. The really funny part was that every seven years, Galactic-Credit-Cark-It made all of the houses on their planets fall down. Then, all of the pigs on those planets became narcissistic and consumed everything, even sometimes themselves. But you know what the really, really funny part was?"

"Enlighten me."

"Each planet had accepted only five refugees in every two gazillion."

"What a riot." *Not.*

"Well, according to the Guidelines, since you haven't read the book, I've concluded that you lack self-awareness."

Strike a light, I think it was right. If I really was an all-consuming animal, then I should've been able to turn into a werewolf. But like I said, I couldn't. Then the pig concentrated on the computer screen and it narrowed its eyes and looked confused. I felt like biting its hind leg but I held back 'cos those guards with their laser guns were standing behind it.

"You forgot to say how much money you have," the pig said.

"A gazillion dollars," I said.

"Where from?"

"Pokies-In-Space."

The pig's face scrunched up. "I'm tired of all you rich wolves jumping from planet to planet, being too picky even though you've been granted asylum somewhere else. Then you all turn up in these rickety old space shuttles."

"So what, mate? A wolf's gotta do what a wolf's gotta do."

I took out my one gazillion dollar Pokie-In-Space chip. "Why don't you have this," I said, and winked with my right eye. I put it on the counter and the pig pushed it back towards me. It squinted its eyes.

"Anyways, the Guidelines state you need a gazillion dollars to the power of ten, so you don't qualify."

Suddenly, from behind me I heard this noisy racket. I turned around and there was a bunch of animals walking on their hind legs all dressed in floral shirts and they all had zinc suncream on their noses. Flamin' hell, was there a beach around here? There were horses, cows, donkeys, goats and get this, a skunk! One of the horses was carrying a replica boogie board and the skunk had a replica pair of yellow floaties around its front legs. They all walked through the checkpoint without even being questioned. Then, there was a PA announcement:

"ATTENTION, ATTENTION! All you animals (except you, Mr Wolf) are welcome. Please spend all of your money and help increase our credit rating and don't overstay your visas, or else."

"*Ooohhh* — fair crack of the whip, mate," I said.

"Oh, wait a second . . . I recognise that accent of yours," the pig said, scratching its head. "Hold on, I know it, where have I heard that strange accent before?"

"It's *Ostrayan*, mate," I said. Could you believe it? I was being discriminated against. "By the way, did you just say *anyways* a second ago — who taught you English?"

The pig rolled its eyes. "That's it! You're not getting a beautiful house of sticks."

Was this clown jokin'? Was this dump beautiful? This was worse than a zoo.

"Look, I could be of use to you . . . I used to kill mutant pigs," I said.

"Really? That's so cools."

Cools. The nong couldn't even speak proper English, let alone *Ostrayan*.

"If anything turns up, I'll let management know," the pig said. "But don't bother huffing and puffing. Get lost."

I wasn't even gonna try. So I rolled my eyes.

"Don't give me lip, you!"

"Stuff youse then," I said, and headed back to the space shuttle with my tail between my legs.

Chapter Two: To the Planet of Sticks

Questions for consideration

4. In which ways has Big Bad Ben, the refugee wolf, been stopped from entering the Planet of Straw and the Planet of Sticks?

5. In response to the pig which says, "I'm tired of you rich wolves jumping from planet to planet, being too picky even though you've been granted asylum somewhere else. Then you all turn up in these rickety old space shuttles"; Big Bad Ben says, "So what, mate? A wolf's gotta do, what a wolf's gotta do." What is meant by this statement by Big Bad Ben and how does it relate to the discussion about asylum seekers and refugees?

6. On what basis should society restrict, if at all, the flow of immigrants (including asylum seekers and refugees) into a country? Discuss related issues such as population growth, the economy, environment, immigration and human rights law, culture and the history of race relations in your country.

Chapter 3

To the Planet of McSpaceMansions

I was at my lowest point. Fair dinkum, what did they want me to do? Climb onto the roof of this hangar, and wave a placard saying "Save Refugee Wolf" and hopefully get onto Space-Funny News? Was I so desperate that I wanted to live with these ratbags? Yes!

I snapped out of it 'cos my worms were flarin' up again, so I hopped back onto the space shuttle. We headed off to the Planet of McSpaceMansions. I had heard they had houses that were small on the outside and mega-gigantic on the inside. Apparently, everything was in there: shopping malls within shopping malls within shopping malls, hotels, casinos, villages, swimming pools, yellow brick roads, and that was only in one McSpaceMansion. You didn't have to go out at all to meet anyone. Well, I guess if they accepted me as a refugee

I *could* live in one, as long there was a pub. As we descended, I looked outside of the window and the McSpaceMansions' white coats of paint beamed brightly. It was hard to tell them apart from each other.

We landed. As I walked down the steps onto the tarmac, the flight attendant asked, "Hey, maybe we can catch up some day?"

"No worries," I said. "Maybe a beer?"

"You know where I am, good luck."

I winked at her and headed to a hangar, again. It was the same set up as on the other planets with the warning sign about watching out for refugee wolves. But this time, there was no side area in order to fill in a form. I walked up to the counter.

Behind it was a pig — but get this — it had *two* heads and grey hair cut into a bob on each head; on its left forehead was tattooed with the words "We're Not Full", while its right forehead was tattooed with "We're Full". Anyway, it wore a floral jumpsuit with a red cardigan. Its face was wrinkled but pleasant-looking and kinda reminded me of my nanna.

"G'day," I said. "Just so I understand things around here — is your planet full or not full of pigs?"

"What do you think?"

"I'm a half glass full kind of wolf."

"Well, our Guidelines are here, well, er, to guide us . . . They ensure our world is kept warm and fuzzy and, you know — "

"— Not as furry as me?"

The two-headed pig looked unimpressed and rolled its eyes. "Listen, if you don't shut up, Mr Wolf, I'm going to send you to jail."

So touchy.

"Now, let's get to the point," the two-headed pig said. "The only criteria you need to satisfy is whether you're on Spacebook. Now, are you?"

"*Maaaaaate*, rack off," I said.

"You're *soooo* missing out — I love it. I'm on it all the time. On Spacebook you can consume all of your friends' lives, replay them, pretend to be someone else and pick up hot dates, watch your friends going to the toilet, and read great books like *Inter-Galactic Naysayers* . . ."

"No way."

"And you know the best thing of all?"

"What?"

"I can consume all of this on my MicroTab which is built into my two brains — every pig on our planet is programmed this way . . ."

The *flamin'* idiot went on and on and on. To my left, a few metres away, was a long cylindrical metal tube. It had a green glow, too. I walked up to it and noticed there was a small label on it.

The label read:

WHAT'S THE TIME, MR WOLF? TIME TO GO BACK TO WHERE YOU CAME FROM!

Fair dinkum. I was still thinking about the skunk. I might have been bad, but not smelly. Then, I looked through the glass and out into the distance where there were gazillions of McSpaceMansions. The two-headed pig was still rabbiting on as I walked back to the counter.

"Look, mate, I'd rather be at the pub with my mates inhaling a few cold ones," I said.

"So old fashioned," the two-headed pig said. "Well, the Guidelines state that if you want to come here you have to fight the Biggest, Baddest Wolf of them all. It's called Fang-sta."

"You're jokin' . . ."

"It's a robot and ten times the size of you. It's programmed to react to fear. But Fang-sta's also a prankster."

"A galah, eh?" Bet you it wasn't funnier than me.

Anyway, no prankster was gonna make me skid my tracky dax. I had watched a lot of reruns of Kung Fu films and knew a few killer moves. I *loved* Kung Fu.

"Righto, bring it on, luv," I said.

"You think you can take it?"

"Yeah, she'll be right."

"Have you seen *Chop Socky Wolf*?" the two-headed pig said.

"Mate, is that meant to be a trick question?" I said. "You a fan?"

"Love him — watched it a gazillion times on my MicroTab," the two-headed pig said.

I was impressed with the porker. I never would've thought I'd have anything in common with a pig. Especially a two-headed one.

"*Goodonyaluv*, just watch me belt the living daylights out of it," I said.

The Battle of the Biff took place in this huge boxing ring. The two-headed pig pressed a button on the counter. Up from under the floor behind me a boxing ring bobbed up. Fangsta stepped into the ring and stood about ten metres away in the red corner. It was a *tank* with a long tail. There were dry blood stains on the canvas. I smelt the blood of my own kind as I stepped into the blue corner. *Strewth*, once I saw

Fang-sta's big iron paws, I soiled my tracky dax.

The security guards surrounded the ring and more came to make up a crowd of about two hundred pigs. A few fired their laser guns in the air and they all chanted in a high-pitched tone: "Faaaang-sta, we love you praaaankster, Faaaang-sta, we love you praaaanskter . . ." The loud cheering echoed throughout the hangar.

I hardly heard the ding of the bell and Fang-sta leapt out and jabbed with its left paw, just missing me. *Ratbag.* It growled and I stepped towards it. I skipped and bobbed my head every now and again. I jumped about two metres in the air and tried returning a jab with my right paw but missed because it was too tall. It jabbed again with its left paw, just clipping my chin. I quickly ran up close and tried to do a reverse sweep with my right leg but in the middle of my move, it clubbed me with its right paw. I went down like a bag of spuds which made my gut rumble. Lying down semi-unconscious, I said, "Hold on, big fella." I gestured with my paws for a time out. The umpire — a pig with only one eye and dressed in a black silk kimono — ushered Fang-sta back into its corner.

I got back up, and pranced around and poked my tongue out. Fang-sta came out and growled.

Grrr . . . I stopped. Next, I tried the Zippy Hind Leg of the Wolf move but the ratbag was onto that as soon as I tried to rotate my left leg in the air like a rotor. It didn't surprise me when its tail turned into a wet towel and flicked my bottom. Ouch!!! Fang-sta laughed at me like a cockatoo — the nong. The rumble in my gut was getting louder.

The two-headed pig was watching me and drifted into my corner of the ring. I was bloody and bruised and could barely see. I slowly walked over to the corner. I heard the two-headed pig's sweet voice that sounded like my nanna.

"Do you remember the scene in *Chop Socky Wolf* where the master teaches his student a move but he gets it wrong, and then the master kicks him up the bum and says, 'Release your inner howl'"?

"Yeah."

"Well, stop mucking around and be an animal!" the two-headed pig said.

Strewth, why didn't I think of that? I closed my eyes and tried channelling the moon but nothing happened. I heard Fang-sta's legs pounding the canvas; it came closer. Then, I had a great idea — stuff this self-awareness mumbo-jumbo. Somehow, my worms stopped wriggling around and I felt there was a clear passage. The biggest rip snorter of a fart was coming on. I let it rip. Fang-sta took one whiff and carked it.

I stepped out of the ring. The two-headed pig winked at me but suddenly I heard an alarm go off. From behind the counter a group of guards came out of a door carrying those laser guns and lined up around the ring. It was announced on the PA that Omni-Vortexa was going to intervene. It came through the door.

Flamin' hell, I couldn't believe it. It was a robot and had three heads. Just like the two-headed pig, its left forehead was tattooed with "We're Not Full", while its right forehead had the words, "We're Full". Its middle forehead was tattooed with the word, "Bouncer".

It was about a foot taller than me and carried in its left trotter an old-school replica 1980s-style ghetto blaster which blared out a synthesised rap beat: tukka-tukka-tuh, tuh-tuh, tukka-tukka-tuh, tuh-tuh . . . at high volume. Omni-Vortexa's silk maroon tracky dax was a tight fit. It had bulging forearms and it wore a gold and diamond chain around its thick neck. The gold shone shards of yellow light, while each five carat diamond beamed bling.

It turned down the blaster and walked up to me and shook my paw — I shook its right trotter.

"Look mate," I said. "I've passed everythin' you've thrown at me. You gonna let me in?"

Omni-Vortexa took a deep breath, and a clanging noise came from inside its steel belly. "Not by the hair of my chinny chin chin."

Strewth, that rhymed.

Then, I thought of my relos from the 1980s on the SCG Hill throwing beer bottles onto the cricket field.

My ears fired up again and I was gonna start huffin' and puffin' but those security guards had their laser guns.

"I loved Fang-sta," Omni-Vortexa said, all teary-eyed. "It was like a son to me."

Strewth, a robotic pig that could cry . . .

"Sorry, boss, didn't mean to cause all this drama," I said.

"Look, I've decided that if you really want to be a part of us we have to de-fang you," Omni-Vortexa said. "Then, you must spend at least a third of a light year in jail — you know, just in case you still have blood-thirsty urges."

"Strewth," I said. My fangs were what made me tick — I wasn't changing for no-one.

"And also, we have to medicate you for that farting problem," Omni-Vortexa said.

"Stone the crows," I said. It may as well have sent me back to Earth.

But then, if I was gonna be here for yonks, I might as well enjoy myself, right?

"Well, if I stay here, I wanna watch *Chop Socky Wolf.*"

"*Huh?*" Omni-Vortexa said.

"Can I suggest something to him?" the two-headed pig said.

The two-headed pig whispered in my ear. "What if I tell Omni-Vortexa you'll promise to listen to the wise words of the Happy Meditator?"

"Just don't let him take my fangs," I said.

"Alright, but you'll have to cut down on pork."

"You're just as tough as my old nanna," I said.

The two-headed pig smiled while Omni-Vortexa stood there with a frown and demanded a response. "*Well?*"

"It's okay. He's going to stay in jail, and listen to a digital recording of the Happy Meditator's mantra. It's called — *I'm a wolf and love veggies,*" the two-headed pig said.

"Alright. But if he misbehaves, de-fang him," Omni-Vortexa said.

Pig's bum I was gonna listen. Well, maybe I would. Depended on if I could scrounge up some beer and get drunk. Omni-Vortexa left with most of his entourage of guards, but a couple of them stuck around.

"Hey, any chance of you getting me Vietnamese pork bread rolls and maybe some beer? Just for old time's sake," I said.

The two-headed pig gestured sideways with its two heads towards the guards. No chance — ratbags. The two guards led me away and we passed behind the counter. We walked through a few corridors down a couple of flights of steps into the basement which contained lots of cells. The cells had rods of blue light which could zap you to death. I saw a few bones lying on the ground, probably wolf bones. As one of the guards pressed a remote control button, a door made of the same rods of blue light slammed. The other guard poked its tongue at me.

I felt like belting them and growled, grrr . . . The guards walked away ahead of the two-headed pig but one of them stopped and said, "Well, at least Omni-Vortexa didn't want you to crawl down the chimney and fall into a pot of boiling hot water, like the ending of *The Three Little Pigs*."

I was lucky, maybe . . . except for the possible radiation.

I sat on a bench and stared at the wall.

About twenty minutes later, the two-headed pig snuck back without any of the guards, carrying a tray with a couple of Vietnamese pork bread rolls, a pot of tea, a can of bickies, a white tablecloth, a six-pack of beer and a remote control. The two-headed pig put the tray down on the floor and pressed the remote and the door opened.

"How did you get the remote?" I said.

"Bribery — told them I'd bake some homemade biscuits with real flour for them."

I smiled. There was a small table that floated in the air. It was situated in the middle of the cell and the two-headed pig set it with the tablecloth and placed everything on it. I was eyeing off the beer.

"Ta, luv. Told you I'd belt it."

I let out a howl and the two-head pig snorted.

"Lucky I've got you, hey?" I said.

"That's okay. If you need more tea, let us know."

"You like pork rolls?" I said, just for a joke.

The two-headed pig stuck out its right trotter, signalling it wanted some. I broke the roll in half and handed it over. The two-headed pig gulped it down and said, "Eat them all the time."

---

[1] This song was written and co-produced by Michael Jackson and produced by Quincy Jones. It was released by Epic Records, September 1987.

[2] *The Three Little Pigs* fairytale can be traced back to *Grimm's Fairy Tales* by the Brothers Grimm, 1812. Later, in 1886, the story appeared in *The Nursery Rhymes of England* by James Orchard Halliwell-Phillips.

Chapter Three:
To the Planet of McSpaceMansions

Questions for consideration

7. Give examples of how colloquial language is used in the story. How is colloquial language used to make the character, Big Bad Ben, like somebody you can relate to?

8. What is the consequence of having a self absorbed, world of excess? How can people be sympathetic towards anyone in this type of world? Despite the story's world of excess and selfishness, the two-headed (nanna) pig tries to help Big Bad Ben; how is this done and why is it important in the story?

9. What are the themes of the story? How are these themes reflected in your society?

Glossary of symbols

Many readers have asked for an explanation of the symbols in Refugee Wolf. The story is written in such a way that there are clues as to what the story is about, but the clues are not completely explained due to the nature of allegory where the symbols and the storyline have to be interpreted.

The story was written on the basis that the debate about asylum seekers — regardless of whether the issue emanates out of Australia or another country — has underlying issues applicable to any part of the world. The debate ebbs and flows, so writing the story "indirectly" through the device of allegory means that readers now, and into the future, can interpret the symbols by researching and analysing the issues relevant to their part of the world to extract the story's meaning.

This glossary is not intended to be the definitive interpretation of the story's symbols. There could well be a number of different interpretations. However, there are likely to be more plausible interpretations as opposed to less feasible ones not consistent with the symbols used.

People in teaching positions may find this glossary as a useful guide.

The following is a list of the main symbols found in the story:

Beer drinking: The wolf (Big Bad Ben), an asylum seeker, escapes from Earth and flies on a space shuttle which has been appropriated by ex-terrorists (who are humans) but who are now helping to smuggle wolves to become refugees. When the wolf arrives on the Planet of Straw, he is firstly rejected for being a beer drinker; then secondly, on the Planet of Sticks he is rejected for not having enough money (even though he has a gambling chip which is worth a gazillion dollars); and thirdly, on the Planet of McSpaceMansions, he is rejected for not subscribing to a social networking site, Spacebook (Facebook). These obstacles symbolise ways in which prejudice can be articulated in society towards people who are foreign, but the story is unclear as to what types of prejudice are at play.

Big Bad Ben: The narrator of the story is a wolf, a knockabout larrikin. He is persecuted for eating too many pigs and becomes a refugee and escapes from the humans who put him in jail. He had once worked for them by eating mutant pigs which landed from outer space at the back of Woop Woop. The words "Big Bad" is derived from the mythology and various fairytales about wolves. The name "Ben" comes from the Michael Jackson song "Ben", written by Don Black and Walter Scharf, Motown 1972. The song was about a boy and his relationship with a rat.

Chop Socky Wolf: This character is a fictional Kung Fu movie which the wolf and the two-headed pig love and have in common. It symbolises the ability of humans to find common ground despite any differences they might have. Martial arts movies usually have a central character who has to overcome obstacles and who experiences a transformation. Likewise, society is arguably capable of transforming and finding common ground.

Excess, the drug/pill: The set-up of the short story is that all of the pigs on the three different planets, (the Planet of Straw, the Planet of Sticks and the Planet of McSpaceMansions) are high on a drug called Excess. They choose to be. The pill is crushed into the water supply and makes all of the pigs have warm and fuzzy thoughts. It symbolises society's complicity in being part of an economic system that only values physical or non physical things that have an economic value. Ironically, in this strange set-up, it is highly unlikely that a wolf would be accepted as a refugee because the pigs are so driven by materialism that they have become too self-absorbed to care about anyone.

Fang-sta the prankster, the robotic wolf: This character symbolises society's heightened fear of people who may be foreign. There are many claims and counter claims in the debate about refugees and immigration. Other issues such as multiculturalism, quality of life, population growth, and the availability of resources are constantly weighed up in the public debate about asylum seekers.

Farts and farting: This device symbolises the heightened emotion of society when discussing asylum seekers and refugees. The farting by the wolf in the story is a crude device in order to produce a comical effect but it makes the reader simultaneously feel that there is something unsettling about the story: perhaps the result of an underlying sensitivity regarding issues such as race or nationality. These issues are never too far from the surface of the public debate about asylum seekers and immigration.

Fight scene between the wolf and Fang-sta, the prankster: This scene symbolises one of the many hurdles any asylum seeker encounters when trying to reach his or her place of asylum regardless of where in the world the claim is made.

Happy Meditator: This character symbolises a cultural figure who can influence society by helping it change its views on asylum seekers through a process of deep reflection and meditation.

LCD signs: There are various physical signs in the story displayed on LCD screens as the wolf tries to gain asylum, for example:

1. "Beware of refugee wolves which say let me in let me in…";
2. "Happy as a pig in mud but we're scared of being swamped by refugee wolves!!!"; and

3. "What's the time, Mr Wolf? Time to go back to where you came from!"

The first sign is an allusion to The Three Little Pigs fairytale where the wolf demands, "Little pig, little pig, let me in let me in…" and a play on the repetitive demand stated by the wolf in the fairytale. This symbolises the desire of refugees to make a claim for asylum. The second reference uses an idiom to highlight the irony of the debate in terms of society wanting a high standard of living and feeling uneasy about feared overcrowding caused by people migrating into their world, regardless of whether they are refugees or not. The third, is an allusion to the children's game where kids ask, "What's the time, Mr Wolf?" As the kids approach the child who pretends to be the wolf, the wolf eventually says, "It's dinner time." These allusions highlight the tension in the asylum seeker debate where some parts of society approve of asylum seekers while others are reluctant to approve of them, or do not do so unconditionally.

Laser guns: The story constantly describes the pigs carrying laser guns on the various planets. For most of the story, the pigs do not fire their guns while the wolf is trying to get into their planet. There is always an implied threat that the laser guns will be used at any time. The only time the laser guns are fired by the pigs is during the fighting scene between the wolf, Big Bad Ben and Fang-sta the prankster, the robotic wolf, because they are excited by the fight. The laser guns symbolise the power of society to use various means to prevent immigration.

LCD screen, glowing with gamma rays: This device symbolises the difficulties asylum seekers face trying to reach their place of asylum in any part of the world.

Masterful Healer: This character symbolises a cultural figure who can engage with the different and competing views of members in society and instill values of fairness and equity into any public debate about asylum seekers.

Minority shareholder pigs which have warm and fuzzy thoughts: The set-up of the story is that there are the super hungry pigs and the minority shareholders, the "everyday" pigs living in the rest of the universe. They make deals with the super hungry pigs to consume more Excess. It is unclear who, in fact, runs the universe. This set-up symbolises how everyone in society is co-opted by a capitalist system into wanting excessive material things because that system constantly urges everyone to produce wealth. There is also the idea that humans are complex creatures whose overall desire to survive and prosper can arguably overshadow other issues, whether it be the environment or any other socially significant issue.

Omni-Vortexa, three-headed robotic pig: This character symbolises society having a debate about population growth and immigration and refugees. On its left forehead is tattooed with the words, "We're Not Full", while its right forehead is tattooed with, "We're Full". Its middle forehead is tattooed with the word "Bouncer". The debate swirls around to every corner of society. The word "Omni" in Latin means all, to be present everywhere, and "Vortex" means a black hole. The two words put together are a play on words, suggesting a dark undertone to the asylum seeker debate.

Planet of McSpaceMansions: In the story of The Three Little Pigs, the last house that the wolf goes to visit is made out of bricks. Rather than using the Planet of Bricks as a concept, the concept of the Planet of McSpaceMansions enlarges the idea of consumption by implying it is pervasive and unrelenting. The use of the concept of McSpaceMansions is a play on the word "McMansion", meaning a big modern house with a lot of rooms and space. They often symbolise over-consumption of resources in the world. This over-consumption arguably renders the world with a reduced ability to be more humane and more thoughtful about the management of resources.

Pokies-in-Space chip: See beer drinking.

Skunk: This minor character symbolises an inconsistency in society's reaction to who is deemed an ideal person to be let in as part of their society. The wolf reflects, towards the end of the story, about why the skunk is allowed into the Planet of Sticks, whereas he is rejected.

Spacebook: See beer drinking.

Super hungry pigs: These animals represent the extremely powerful and wealthy in society.

The Ancient Text of Healing: This is a fictional book in the story used by the Masterful Healer. Refer to the "Masterful Healer".

The ending of the story: The two-headed pig reminds the wolf of his nanna. They do not initially get on with each other. As the story progresses, they find they have something in common, a love of Kung Fu and a fictional movie called Chop Sock Wolf. Throughout the story, the wolf is yearning to eat pork. By the end, the two-headed pig visits the wolf in jail and performs an act of kindness by bringing the wolf a pot of tea, pork rolls and some beer. This symbolises an act of humanity. However, given the two-headed pig lives on a planet of excess consumption — the Planet of McSpaceMansions — a world of houses which are small on the outside, but mega-gigantic on the inside, and which contain "shopping centres within shopping centres within shopping centres", the two-headed pig is co-opted by this excessive consumption.

The wolf says he would be happy in this world of excessive consumption as long there is a pub. All the wolf wants is to be with his mates by sharing a beer with them and having a conversation. He prefers physical contact rather than having his brain, like the two-headed pig, wired into a MicroTab — a computer. On this MicroTab, the two-headed pig enjoys the virtual world of Spacebook, much to the wolf's dismay. The use of the word "Spacebook" is a play on the omnipresence of Facebook. On Spacebook, the two-headed pig says it can consume other pigs' lives by watching it on the MicroTab.

People in society arguably find it difficult to not consume too much given there is no other alternative economic system which balances out competing forces in society in relation to the issue of exploiting resources. They also find it difficult not being on social media for fear of missing out, hence they are less likely to have time for physical engagement with others. By the end of the story, it is unexpected that the two-headed pig likes to eat other pigs — not literally, but there is dark humour at play. The two-headed pig says in the last line of the story that it "eats pork rolls all the time". Its eating of the pork roll is symbolic of a human world of excessive consumerism and a disconnected reality.

The Inter-Galactic Naysayers: This a fictional book referred to in the story. The story refers to the Top Twenty Planets of Excess which allow only five refugees in every two gazillion to enter their world. It symbolises the greatest economic powers on Earth and how they drive the agendas of the world. It is not suggested that the richest countries do not have legal responsibilities for refugees. In the context of the story, they are responsible for dealing with the consequences of materialism and consumerism which can arguably overshadow important issues in society.

The Three Little Pigs: Refugee Wolf is partly inspired by this famous fairytale which can be traced back to Grimms' Fairytales by the Brothers Grimm, 1812 and later The Nursery Rhymes of England by James Orchard Halliwell-Phillipps, 1886. The fairytale's moral is about how three heads, when put together, are better than one. Refugee Wolf is allegorical and the story requires readers to interpret the moral of the story — which is, if society consumes too much, it is unlikely to care about the world and its people, let alone asylum seekers or refugees.

Two-headed pig, the nanna pig: This character symbolises the humane aspect of society. At the end of the story, the two-headed pig brings a pot of tea, Vietnamese pork rolls and beer to the wolf. The two-headed pig reminds the wolf of his nanna and has something in common with the wolf — their love of the great, fictional martial arts movie, Chop Socky Wolf. The idea is that people can try to find things in common to foster debate and acceptance of each other.

Wolf: This character symbolises the ambivalence that society has towards asylum seekers and refugees. It is arguable that society has a sliding scale of sympathy and empathy, and has different depths of concern and fear about asylum seekers and refugees.

Wolf's fangs: At the beginning of the story, the wolf reflects upon how good its fangs look in the mirror. Later in the story, the wolf says that its fangs are "what makes him tick". By the end of the story, the wolf is scared it might have its fangs pulled out by the pigs if it gets into trouble. This symbolises the struggles of a foreign person who migrates and feels compelled to fit into society. Ultimately, however, it is probably what most immigrants — whether they are refugees or not — feel obliged to do.

Worms in wolf's bum: The worms symbolise a troubling issue that never really goes away, supporting the contention that society struggles with an underlying feeling of unease about people who are foreign to them.

Acknowledgements

Thank you to my parents. My late dad, Hai Ngoc Luong, was a persecuted journalist during the Vietnam War. He inspired me to write everything I have written in the last few years. And to my mum, Linda Dang, who has tirelessly supported my sister, Yung, and other family members over the years, thank you for supporting me and putting me in touch with Vietnamese culture and tradition.

Many thanks to the writers and journalists at UTS who taught me during the Masters of Arts in Creative Writing and Bachelor of Arts in Communication. Over the years, you all inspired me and gave me support to write this story and many other pieces of writing and journalism. Many thanks to Debra Adelaide, Mark Rossiter, Jean Beadford, Camilla Nelson, Matthew Dabner, Barbara Brooks, Kirsten Tranter, Adam Aitken, Anthony Macris, Wendy Bacon, Seamus Phelan, David McKnight, Jeannie Martin, Amanda Lohrey and the late Glenda Adams.

Special thanks to my fellow UTS classmates

and writers who provided feedback during the Masters program. After I graduated from the Masters, Kitty Bucholtz became a fantastic mentor because of her unswerving enthusiasm for the craft of writing. Susanna Freymark and Kim Buddee, you both inspired me by your books. Karen Crawshaw, Tom Chapman, Alicia Thompson, Ari Mattes, Jeremy Aitken, Jacqui Moreno-Ovidi, Polly Brennan, Danny Loch, Jacqui Wise, Rebecca Lean and Vi Phan, you were generous with your comments and made me believe in myself.

Thank you to the teaching staff and lawyers at UNSW who gave me an exceptional legal education.

Special thanks to the lawyers at the Arts Law Centre who gave me helpful guidance.

To my high school teachers, Hilary Dixon (year 7–12, French), Debbie Fennell (year 7–10, English and History) and Rhonda Morgan (year 11–12, English), thank you for believing in me and giving me much encouragement.

To my writer friend, Jesse Fink, thank you for making me a better writer and helping me edit my articles over the years. Also, many thanks to my writer friend, Rob Ashton, for proofreading and providing feedback on early drafts of various stories.

Thank you to Gerald Gallagher for your rhyming slang and sense of humour and reminding me that laughter is medicine for the soul.

Thank you to my artist friend, Phil Looney. In 2004, we made a short film for Tropfest which led to the creation of Flying Pig Media, my media entity. You helped me believe that pigs could fly.

To Ian Wilson, Brian Han, Dr Con Papacosta, Jimmy Waldau, Thuy Tran, Lan Bui, Rachael Cunliffe, Michael Strahan, Chris Tsovolos, Denni Fourfouris, Abram Horowitz, Dale Sinnott, Anthony Boutros, Steven Kemp and Maurice Tagliano, David Lau, Caroline Cox, Rod Morrison, Frank and Val Vassal, John Holland and the late Roger Quinn, thank you for your love and warm friendship. You have all travelled with me on life's long journey and we have shared many experiences, stories and memories together.

To the publishing team at Xoum, including Rod Morrison for his inspired leadership and Roy Chen for a brilliant book design and illustration, thank you for all your efforts. Many thanks to my editor, Helen Richardson, for her careful editing.

Big thanks and love to my children, who reminded me of the importance of fairytales, and to my wife for supporting me over the years. Without your love and tireless belief in me I would not be able to achieve anything.